COUNTRY ROAD ABC

COUNTRY ROAD
ABC

AN ILLUSTRATED JOURNEY
THROUGH AMERICA'S FARMLAND

ARTHUR GEISERT

HOUGHTON MIFFLIN BOOKS FOR CHILDREN
HOUGHTON MIFFLIN HARCOURT
BOSTON NEW YORK
2010

Copyright © 2010 by Arthur Geisert

All rights reserved. For information about permission
to reproduce selections from this book, write to
Permissions, Houghton Mifflin Harcourt Publishing Company,
215 Park Avenue South, New York, New York 10003.

Houghton Mifflin Books for Children is an imprint of
Houghton Mifflin Harcourt Publishing Company.

www.hmhbooks.com

The text of this book is set in Bookman BT.
The illustrations were created using copperplate etchings that were hand
colored with acrylic and watercolor on Rieves BFK paper. Dutch Mordant
acid used in the etching process.

Library of Congress Cataloging-in-Publication Data is on file.
ISBN 978-0-547-19469-1

Printed in China
LEO 10 9 8 7 6 5 4 3 2 1
4500202851

To my neighbors,

the people of

letter X

who provided the

visual and technical

information

in this book

A

is for **ammonia fertilizer**

B

is for **barn cats**

C is for coffee and candy

D is for **disking**

E

is for **erosion**

F

is for **fencing**

G

is for
**grinding
feed**

H

is for hay

I is for inoculate

J is for July 4

K

is for kick

L

is for **loading**

M 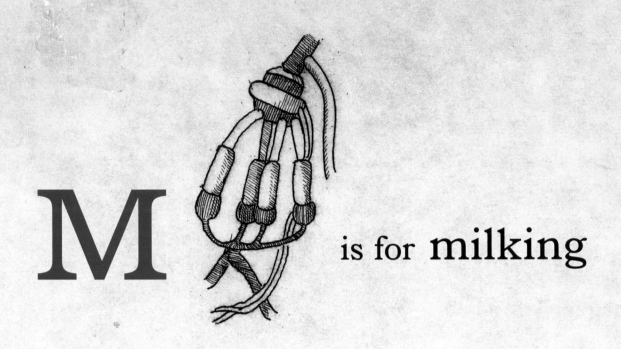 is for milking

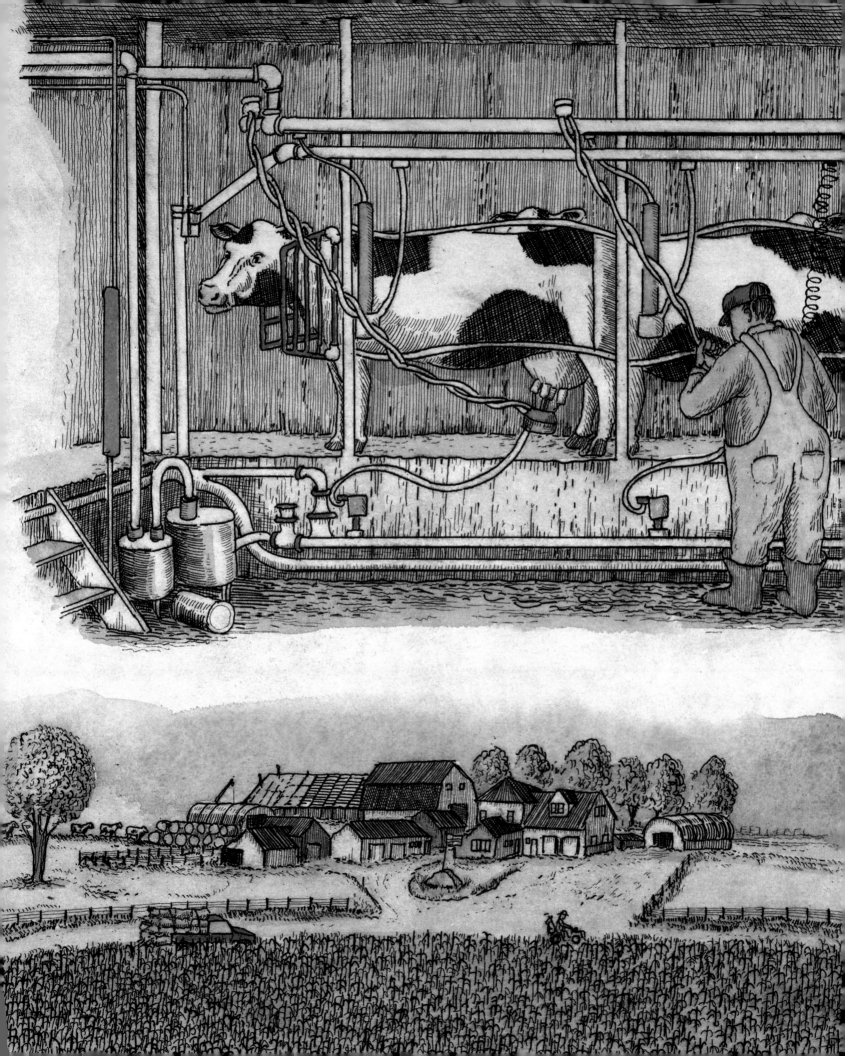

N  is for **no mail today**

O

is for **oat delivery**

P

is for **pigs**

Q is for quicksand

R is for rust

S is for **steel roofing**

T is for traffic

U

is for **uphill**

V is for volunteer fire department

W is for winter afternoon

X

is for **X** marks the spot:
lat. 42° 18' 49" N,
long. 90° 49' 52" W
on County Road Y31

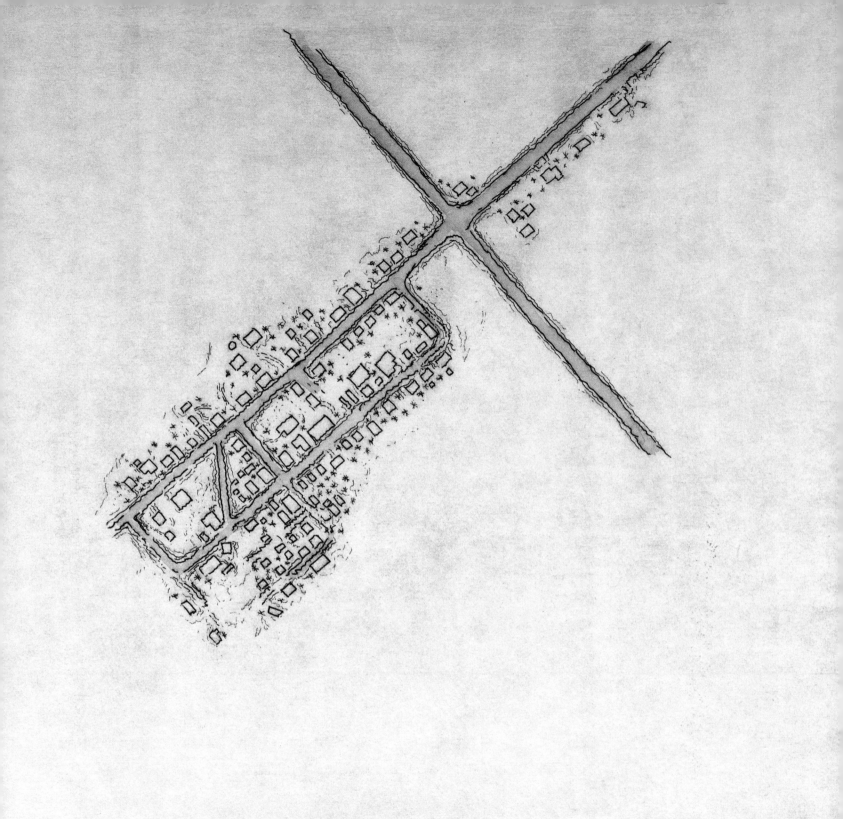

Y is for County Road Y31

Z

is for **z-brace**

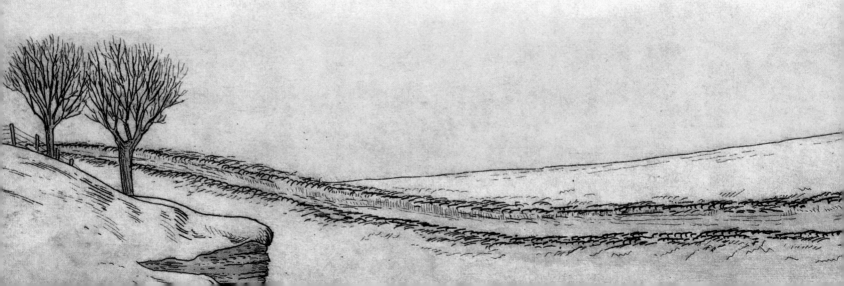

A Farm Glossary

Farmers use **AMMONIA FERTILIZER** to help prepare the soil for planting—the ammonia provides nitrogen for the soon-to-be-planted corn seeds.

BARN CATS help rid the area of mice, who can be destructive to food supplies.

Before a busy day on the farm or after school, it's nice to catch up with friends over **COFFEE AND CANDY** at the local diner.

DISKING is a method of turning over soil in preparation for the planting of oats, corn, and soybeans.

If the spring rains are heavy, a crop can suffer from **EROSION** when the dirt washes away.

Farmers use **FENCING** to distinguish property lines and to keep their animals where they belong. Most fencing is barbed wire.

Many farmers **GRIND** their own **FEED** for the animals on their farms.

HAY is a grass that has been cut and dried, and it is used to feed grazing animals such as cattle, sheep, goats, and horses.

In order to keep the pigs free from disease, a farmer has to **INOCULATE** his animals. (The red spray paint is to keep track of who has been given a shot already!)

Everyone loves a parade on **JULY 4**, our nation's Independence Day.

Cows aren't always friendly—if you get too close, you might get a **KICK**.

There is a lot of **LOADING** on a farm: loading cattle, loading hay, loading feed, loading supplies, all to be transported elsewhere.

Machinery now does the **MILKING** of cows on most farms.

When it is **OAT DELIVERY** day, farmers can count on being itchy all over from the dust and chaff, which is the outside casing of the oat.

Another quiet day in the countryside: **NO MAIL TODAY,** but maybe tomorrow.

PIGS are found on many farms in the United States and are very intelligent animals.

The jungle's not the only place you can find **QUICKSAND**—it can develop on a farm when water collects on top of a hard top layer of soil. The water turns the soil into a squishy mess capable of swallowing half a tractor.

Between rain, wind, and sun, items lined up in a yard, covered in **RUST,** are a common sight in the farmland. Every farm has a junk pile.

Farmers put up **STEEL ROOFING** to protect their barns from leaks—the steel has been gradually replacing wood as a building material.

You won't see the same kind of **TRAFFIC** jam here that you'll see in the big city—you are more likely to be stuck behind a slow-moving piece of farm machinery with a top speed of eighteen miles per hour.

UPHILL—it's where the schoolhouse used to be located. Both ways, of course.

Some farmers are also members of the **VOLUNTEER FIRE DEPARTMENT,** an integral part of the community as there is not a full-time fire department.

There's not always a lot to do on a **WINTER AFTERNOON** in the country—except maybe play some cards and drink some coffee.

X MARKS THE SPOT. It's as simple as that.

The way in and out of the farmland, the road to and from the city, and the road on which supplies are delivered is **COUNTY ROAD Y31**.

If you want your barn doors to stand the test of time, you are going to want to build them using a sturdy **Z-BRACE**.

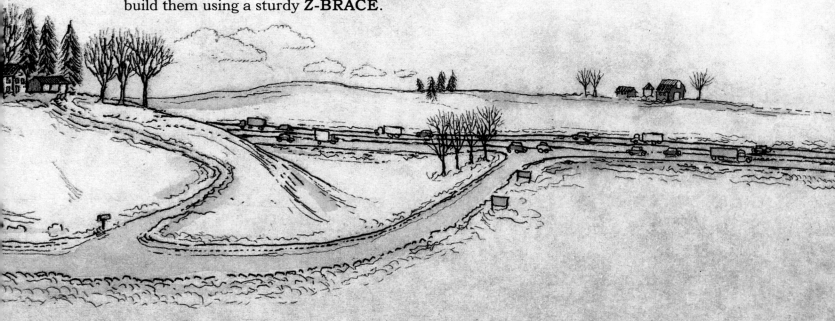

ACKNOWLEDGMENTS

A THANK-YOU TO THE OWNERS OF THE SITES AND FARMS
DEPICTED IN THE ILLUSTRATIONS:

Leonard and Deb Ambrosy
Lori Cook
Kevin and Darlene Curoe
Shirley Curoe
Jay and Marlene Decker
Larry and Lynn Decker
Loras and Rita Federspiel
Harold and Joyce Gibbs
Melvin and Rose Henneberry
Ron and Jody Kenneally
William and Janell Klosterman
Carl Kurt and Carla Kurt
Whitey Reiter and Margie Larkin
Robert McKenna
Louis and Betty Meyerhoff
Dick and Barb Molony
Rich and Kelly Molony
Bob and Vicki Noonan
Chuck and Amy Noonan
John and Mary Pat Noonan
Dave and Mary Puetz
Pat and Ruth Rea
Bones Reiter
Rick and Emily Roling
Tom and Cheri Ryan
Larry Simon
Gary and Patti Steffen

Interiors:
"Coe's Bar" — Ron and Jody Kenneally
"Pearl's Place" — Carol Shanahan